When an ancient evil came to Keblear Township, only Tearn Alder, the fourth son of his storied House, recognized it for what it was.

Too bad nobody believed him. He had time to escape. He could have run. Instead, Tearn took up his sword to stand alone against the darkness. Must he sacrifice his soul to save his town, or is the town's fate already sealed?

The Keblear Horror is a short story (~5,200 words) set in the same world as Glenn G. Thater's acclaimed epic fantasy series, Harbinger of Doom.

BOOKS BY GLENN G. THATER

THE HARBINGER OF DOOM SAGA
GATEWAY TO NIFLEHEIM
THE FALLEN ANGLE
KNIGHT ETERNAL
DWELLERS OF THE DEEP
BLOOD, FIRE, AND THORN
GODS OF THE SWORD
THE SHAMBLING DEAD
MASTER OF THE DEAD
SHADOW OF DOOM
WIZARD'S TOLL
VOLUME 11+ *forthcoming*

THE HERO AND THE FIEND
(A novelette set in the Harbinger of Doom universe)

THE GATEWAY
(A novella length version of *Gateway to Nifleheim*)

HARBINGER OF DOOM
(Combines *Gateway to Nifleheim* and *The Fallen Angle* into a single volume)

THE DEMON KING OF BERGHER
(A short story set in the Harbinger of Doom universe)

THE KEBLEAR HORROR
(A SHORT STORY SET IN THE HARBINGER OF DOOM UNIVERSE)

To be notified about my new book releases and any special offers or discounts regarding my books, please join my mailing list here: http://eepurl.com/vwubH

GLENN G. THATER

THE

KEBLEAR

HORROR

A TALE FROM THE
HARBINGER OF DOOM SAGA

THE KEBLEAR HORROR © 2016 by Glenn G. Thater

ISBN-13: 978-0692651131
ISBN-10: 0692651136

Visit Glenn G. Thater's website at
http://www.glenngthater.com

February 2016 Edition
Published by Lomion Press

THE KEBLEAR HORROR

KEBLEAR TOWNSHIP KINGDOM OF LOMION

THE 4TH AGE OF MIDGAARD

TEARN ALDER

I crept into the cave undetected and alone. Despite the small, hidden entrance, the creatures had kept two sentries on duty all day and into the night, but I snuck past them. I was probably the only man in the village who could enter unseen into that frightful place, do what must be done, and have any hope of coming out alive. No doubt, to some, my assertion sounds like a boast, but I maintain the truth of it. You see, not long before his passing, old Master Galuck trained me in the arts of combat, stealth, and tracking, and that was after years of instruction under my father's best men-at-arms and woodsmen. No doubt, you recognize Galuck's name and have some sense of his reputation, even if you can't place him.

To my good fortune, the old master retired to our far-flung village after serving for twenty

5

long years as House Alder's Weapons Master in Lomion City, which was four times as long as the most stalwart of his last five predecessors. I'm an Alder myself, by the way. Tearn, fourth son of Tagbert, third cousin to Mother Alder herself.

Over the span of nearly a year, leading up to his death, Master Galuck taught me the Old Way of the Sword. Not the watered-down version gingerly presented to the delicate flowers nowadays. With me, he employed the traditional methods of bygone days when men were made of sterner stuff, body and mind.

The training nearly killed me, and I've got the scars to show for it, but it was worth it. Worth every bruise and scrape, every bucket of sweat and drop of blood.

Galuck's goal: teach me to survive combat. Real combat. Not just a bit of sparring on the tourney field, or a brawl at the promenade.

His methods bore fruit.

I learned how to fight. Far better than our best men-at-arms.

And I learned to kill.

And most importantly, I learned how to avoid being killed.

Galuck said he was pleased with my progress and he was not a man known for loosely tossing complements.

I wasn't the only one who got the training, of course. Galuck taught many men from the village in his last years, my brothers included, but not a one had my martial talents. Or my wits. Or, I daresay, my ambitions. A fourth son has to make his own way in the world, you see. He can't rely on his family name or wealth for much of anything. By longstanding Lomerian tradition, the eldest son inherits almost everything of value. The second son, the rest. Daughters get married off to the rich and powerful to cement alliances and business ventures. Third sons and down, get squat, save for the family name. I carry it proudly. Always have. Always will, though I'll admit, it has caused me no end of troubles. Maybe some commoners and lowlifes have it in for all the noble Houses, or else, mayhap, folks have a special disdain for the Alders. I'm not certain which it is. And I suppose, I don't much care. My rotten luck to be born to a nearly forgotten branch of that great House, and out on the edge of the wild to boot. Better than being a pig farmer, I suppose. Not that there's anything wrong with that.

And so, by the bye, there I found myself. At the mouth of hell.

Or thereabouts. Creeping up on their evil cave, crawling along on my belly, camouflaged of mud, grass, and shrubbery.

My heart raced; blood pounded in my ears. One false move, one kicked stone, or a single crunched leaf, and they'd hear me.

And all my skills notwithstanding, I'd be done for, quick as that.

For the foul demon spawn would be on me in an instant - rending and tearing with their vile, unholy claws, pouring out of their forsaken tunnels en masse to pounce upon me. I wouldn't have a chance. No man deserves such a death, least of all, an honest and god-fearing man such as me.

But I had to do that thing, I had to get into their lair, however grave the danger, however foolish the very notion.

I had to protect my village.

A hero is what the village needed. And that's what I aimed to be. That would be my deliverance from mediocrity. My first chance in life to make something of myself. To do something important. Something great.

The things that dwelt in that cave, horrors out of hell that they were, arrived nary one month prior, though already it seemed an eternity that they'd plagued us. Where they came from, whether conjured by some mad witch from the White Wood, or a curse unleashed by a mage out of the Eastmors, no man can say. Perhaps they burrowed up from eerie subterranean depths of their own accord or mayhap they tumbled down upon a dark star cast out of the heavens by the gods themselves.

All I can say for certain is that one month

ago they arrived and overran the foreboding hill beyond the old cemetery. They dug their warrens deep into the earth in the dark of night, all the while, hiding from the eyes of man and god and the cleansing rays of blessed sunlight. They crafted an unholy laboratory within those unseen depths, and hidden within, they concocted a dark elixer -- a plague of evil never before known on Midgaard, the world of man. Those dark fiends sought not to do battle with us, or to tempt us with wealth or wishes and steal our immortal souls, as any honest demons would. Instead, they strove to take us unawares by foul poison -- a crafty coward's weapon. That evil I could not suffer. Not even if moving against them would cost me my very life. Or my immortal soul.

Each morning, soon after the arrival of those creatures, when the goodly townsfolk emerged from their homes to go about their daily toils, they - one and all -- whether owner of a rickety hovel on Broad Street or a well-kept mansion on Long Hill Way, would find a malefic meal neatly arranged on their doorsteps: a silky brown poison created in some dark demoniac cauldron and spread meticulously upon an alluring confection that tempted the palate and confounded the mind.

What could be their plan, but for some hungry child to step out to play, snatch that poison thing up, and put it to their mouths? Or for some foolish adult to do the same? Those fiends sought to slay us all on our very porches.

To cloak their treachery, they formulated a devil's cake that did no harm to animals -- for when family pets or a hungry squirrel or raccoon or other such beast of the field partook of the deadly feast, it did them no grievous harm.

I was not to be fooled by such trickery, for I knew the minds of those monsters of old. Legends that stretched back to the most distant memories, to the most ancient tales of the Volsung people, told of those creatures of chaos. Monsters that skulked uninvited into homes at night, that stole babies from their cribs and replaced them with the malformed fruit of their own vile loins.

And so a warrior, a hero, was needed to skulk about in the night and creep unseen into the unnatural tunnels beneath Cemetery Hill. There, to mark those minions of chaos, and put an end to their unholy reign of terror.

Such was my mission. My purpose. My calling.

Hours before I made my way into that god-forsaken cave, by happenstance, I met my brothers in town as I foraged for a morning meal. Old Thom the cobbler had offered me the two cakes left on his doorstep that morning. I wouldn't touch them, of course, and was holding out for one of the fresh-baked loaves of rye his wife was famous for. Thom's grandmother, Old Nan the village healer, ancient and wizened even when my grandmother was but a wee girl, sat in her rocking chair outside the cobbler shop and urged Thom to gift me the bread and to throw away those rotten cakes. "I'll get you a cup of sage tea with honey to wash the bread down," she said as she struggled out of her chair mumbling that I looked half dead. "That will perk you up and straighten out your head," she said as she stepped inside.

"Tearn," shouted Teal as he and Torman jogged towards me. "Are you all right?" he said, his eyes wide, looking me up and down. "What happened?"

"What do you mean?" I said, confused.

"You haven't been home in two days, for Odin's sake," said Teal. "And you look like Helheim. What happened to you?"

"Was it highwaymen?" said Torman. "Are you injured?"

It was only then that I realized my disheveled appearance. "I'm fine," I said. "I spent the night reconnoitering Cemetery Hill. The ground was muddy. I'm quite well, actually, considering."

"You spent all night in the cemetery?" said Teal.

"The last two nights," I said.

"He's gone unhinged," said Torman.

"I've been studying their movements," I said. "I've got a good sense of when they come and go, and when they change their guards. I think that I can sneak in. Find out what they're about."

Teal and Torman looked as if they didn't understand me, as if I were speaking a different language. Old Thom pretended he hadn't heard anything and slipped away, cakes still in hand.

"Bandits in the cemetery?" said Torman. "I haven't heard reports of any robberies in town."

"He's talking about Dark Elves," said Teal as he shook his head. "He thinks they're the ones making the cookies. And that they fill them with poison."

"You're not still on about that, are you?" said Torman.

"He told you too?" said Teal.

"He's told everybody," said Old Nan as she emerged from her door with a steaming cup of tea in hand. "Gave the ladies quite a fright about it at services last week. Matron Nisco fainted outright; nearly cracked her skull in the fall. And Matron McKee's little granddaughter Debbie ran crying from the temple. Quite entertaining it was, if you ask me."

Teal's face hardened. "Tearn, you need to get a hold of yourself," he said. "It's one thing to spin your tales of fancy with us, it's another to tell other folk. You could tarnish our House's reputation. We can't have that. There are no monsters lurking up on Cemetery Hill, or anywhere else in the township for that matter. These creatures are but figments of your troubled mind. Now, let's get you home and cleaned up. Then we'll sit down and have a long talk with father."

"I've had that talk, already," I said. "He doesn't believe me any more than you do. He says they're gnome bakers up from Gokell. He says they're giving out free cakes to get everyone hooked on them, then they'll start charging. Smart business people, he marks them. Except, they're not people at all. They're Black Elves. Svarts out of Thoonbarrow. Just like in the old stories. They're here for dark purposes. I'm certain of it. And those cakes are at the heart of it. They'll poison us all if we let them."

"That's just crazy talk," said Teal, as he looked around, as if he were concerned that a crowd might gather to gawk. Bad enough that Old Nan and Thom had heard it all.

"Plenty of folks have seen them," said Torman. "They're Gnomes, not Black Elves. Not that anybody hereabouts would know a Black Elf if they saw them. Those are just fairy stories. Gnomes are Gnomes. That's all they are."

"I know that they look like Gnomes," I said. "But they're wearing disguises. They put on Gnome style clothing, fake beards, and they color their skin. Under it all, they're Black Elves. Skin, black as pitch. Huge dead eyes. Bald heads. No expressions. No emotions. More like things than men."

"How do you know this?" said Teal. "Have you seen them without these disguises on?"

"I've seen enough," I said.

"He hasn't seen anything," said Torman. "You best come home with us, now."

"I suppose that if father were here and he ordered me home, I'd have to comply," I said. "But he's not. So I won't. I'm my own man. And I'll do as I see fit. Will you help me or not?"

"Help you do what?" said Teal.

"Expose their plot," I said. "Prove that they're Black Elves and up to no good."

"And then?" said Teal. "What are you going to do, murder them?"

"If they are Black Elves," I said, "that's exactly what I'll do. But I'll need help for that. There are more of them then you'd believe. A few score at the least."

"A few score?" said Torman. "I figured it was one baker and his family; probably with several sons and daughters. A dozen or so in the clan, all considered. Can't be many more than that."

"I've seen a good deal more than that, whether you believe it or not," I said. "Will you help me or no?"

Teal considered for some moments, before answering. "Collect your evidence," he said. "Be home by nightfall tonight and tell us your findings. We'll review it together, as a family, and set a course of action. In the meantime, don't dare act against them. Don't hurt a single hair on their heads. We don't want to give away that we're watching them. Agreed?"

I beamed. My smile so wide that it hurt. "I agree. I'll see you tonight."

And my brothers were on their way, though the looks of concern never left their faces. Old Nan gifted me a wink and a nod as she retook her spot on the rocking chair. She believed me. What a comfort that was, that small gesture. To know that I was not alone. That I was not the only person left in the village not yet bewitched. But still, a crone would be of no help to me in the battle that was coming.

I was surprised that I'd convinced my brothers that I might be right. I half suspected them to knock me down and drag me off home. I guess they realized that they couldn't do that anymore. Not after all my training.

My problems began later that morning when I couldn't gather any useful evidence save for more visual observations. I needed to get inside their warrens to find something I could take back to father and my brothers, to convince them. But there was no way to get inside that place unseen during the day. I had to wait until nightfall. That meant I'd not be home at the agreed upon hour. But it had to be that way. If I went home empty handed, that would be a waste of time for all of us. And if things went against me, father would have me locked in the tower to keep me out of trouble. I had no wish to suffer that humiliation again.

I'd wait until dark and then find a way to slip inside. Then, I'd see what there was to see. I'd bring back the evidence, and then everyone would know the truth. They'd know that I was right. That my vigilance had saved the town. And then we'd rise up against those devils and give them what for. I'd fight at my father's side at last. My brothers with us. The Alder banner proudly waving over us. They'd be proud of me, all of them. Together, we'd send those Black Elves back down to Thoonbarrow, screaming for their lives.

A couple of thrown pebbles is all it took for me to gain entry to the Elves' lair. The sounds of them cascading through the brush in the otherwise silent cemetery distracted the guards, moved them off their perches to check out what went on. And then I skulked right into the cave, silent as death, just like old master Galuck had taught me. I prayed as I entered that there were no Elves lying in wait. It was a gamble. A great risk. The mouth of that cave might've opened into a chamber, filled with who knows how many of those fiends. But it didn't. It was a tunnel. Long and dark and dank, and angled ever downward. Many smaller tunnels branched off the main, this way and that. My instincts told me to avoid them, head down the main tunnel. That's where I'd find my answers.

My hair stood on end the whole time. My nerves, frayed. Sweat dripped off me. And with every step, I expected the Elves to appear out of the darkness and accost me. Their disguises doffed. Those large, alien eyes boring into me. Those claws. Teeth. And who knows what else.

I don't know how long I walked that tunnel. It might've been only a minute or two. It might've been ten, or even more, the darkness broken only by the occasional candle hung in a wall sconce. Some small consolation was that light. At least I'd see them coming. Have some hope to defend myself. To give as good as I got. I kept my sword close at my side, though I still hoped beyond hope to avoid detection.

And then at last, I heard sounds up ahead. Many voices. And metallic sounds, as if from a smithy or a kitchen. I knew that I couldn't walk openly into that room and hope to ever walk out again. So I headed down the nearest side tunnel. It angled upward just before the main corridor opened up into the chamber from which the sounds came. The side corridor went on for a ways, perhaps fifty feet, steeply upward. I had to crawl part of the way, the ceiling so low. At last, I found myself upon a ledge overlooking their main cavern. Still undetected, I barely risked to breathe.

Peeking out from behind a boulder, I watched them go about their evil deeds, and heard them chatter in their high-pitched little voices. But to my surprise, it was not a horde of Black Elves that I surveilled, but a troop of common Gnomes. Nothing but Gnomes. Bright clothes. White beards. Pointy hats. And more.

Was it possible that they maintained their disguises even there, deep within their secret cavern system? Or were they truly only Gnomes?

Master Galuck had taught me to always trust my instincts. Sometimes, he said, the eyes can be tricked, the nose can be fooled, the ears can be deceived, but our instincts are ever honest and true.

All my instincts screamed out for caution. They told me I looked upon an evil the like of which had never before infested my beloved town. These were not Gnomes. These were the dreaded Svarts of ancient horror tales. Creatures that crawled up from the Nether Realms to plague mankind, to destroy us. Evil incarnate. Every fiber of my body cried out that that is what I looked upon, my eyes be damned.

And so I studied them in their ponderous cavern. I watched and I waited as the hellions worked an array of blasphemous machines that spewed smoke and steam and made queer sounds. The heat within the place was oppressive, for huge iron ovens, one after another, were all afire along one wall. No doubt, within those furnaces, they planned to cook us, one and all, after we succumbed to their poisons.

I watched as they poured their demonic, soupy mix onto big metal trays, and slid them into the ovens for baking. From other ovens, they pulled trays brimming with the finished products -- cakes, cookies, and confections of all manner and description. Sprinkled atop and within some of them were dark blots of their foul brown poison -- which was a liquid when heated but quickly solidified to a hardened substance when cooled. The smell of their evil confections was pleasant and sweet and filled the air. Those demon treats, if you will, had an allure to them -- both to the eyes and to the nose. They drew one in. But that was their evil magic, was it not? I would not be fooled.

As I watched, mesmerized, from out of the shadows stepped their scrawny leader. A bespectacled graybeard with a pointy hat. It directed its minions about their work, and urged on their madness, whipping them into a demoniac frenzy.

I knew then what I must do, though it would cost me my very life. If I could but destroy their leader, cut him down here and now, it may well be the end of this. Without him, the others may scurry back whence they came, and my town would be safe and free of them at last. And this might be my only chance. The town's only chance.

But it meant that I would never achieve my ambitions -- not in life, but mayhap, in death. For in days to come, my name would be remembered with honor and my tale of bravery and sacrifice would long be told. Not many fourth sons could claim such renown. Perhaps then, my father would be proud.

I could debate myself no more, for if I continued, fear might overcome me. I might be paralyzed with fright. Unable to act. I had to move. Now. I stood up boldly, and with a mad yell, the war cry of House Alder escaped my lips. I leaped down from the ledge, sword in hand. Landed heavily before the demon king itself.

The creature was startled. Stumbled back. Shock on its face. But even as I stepped forward, sword raised in a death stroke, the creature composed itself.

"Hello!" it said with a smile and a pleasant tone that disarmed me and stayed my hand. "Have you come for more cookies? We've just finished a new batch. We've got chocolate chip and oatmeal raisin, all still warm and chewy. I recommend the chocolate chip, but the oatmeal is excellent too."

The fiend could not fool me. "I've come to put this blasphemy to an end," I shouted. I raised my sword anew -- a heavy broadsword it was, straight from the House armory. No storied blade was it. No Dyvers steel. But still, it was honest Lomerian steel, heavy and sharp enough to cut the imp in half.

The monster looked confused. And frightened.

I spied its diminutive minions from the corners of my eyes. They flooded the chamber. Emerged from hidey holes in all directions like roaches. Many held strange weapons that at careless glance looked akin to forks, spatulas, and rolling pins.

"Be calm, sir," said the Svart king, its eyes wide. "Please lower your weapon. We'll give you all the cookies that you want. All that you can eat and more. As much as you can carry. They are free to all goodly folk. No threats are needed. Please, don't hurt us."

"I don't want your stinking devil cookies," I shouted. "I want you gone from here. Leave our town and plague us no more. Swear it or I'll cut you down where you stand."

The old king cringed, cowered in fear. It knew it was outmatched. It could not stand against a nobleman of Lomion. Tears formed in its eyes. "Please, please, sir. Do not hurt me and mine. There are no foes for you to fight here. We are but simple bakers come to share our treats with the good folk of Keblear Town."

"Just bakers? Do not waste your lies on me. I know what you are. You're Svarts, Black Elves out of Thoonbarrow, or some such."

"Sir, we are Gnomes, not Elves," said the king, waving his hands in a panic. "Peaceful Gnomes. Friendly Gnomes. We travel from town to town, baking cookies and cakes for fine Volsung folk like you. That is what we do. All that we do. Please, put down your sword," it said as a tear streamed down its lined face.

I looked around. The other Gnomes all looked concerned. Frightened. Cowed into silence by the plight of their king. Several were crying, as children.

Dear gods, what was I doing? Those little creatures were no threat, any fool could see that. If they had been Black Elves, they would've swarmed me from the first. Blades from all sides. Teeth, claws, and magics unknown. But there was none of that. None. Only the crying. The whimpering. The pleading.

I could not believe what I had almost done. What a fool I had been. What a madman. I had almost cut down a goodly old man for no reason and nothing. My brother was right, my mind is troubled. Father was right to lock me in the tower for all those months. To keep me away from goodly folk. To stop me from hurting people.

What is wrong with me?

I don't even know what's real anymore.

I lowered my sword. No sooner had I done so, than around me the little Gnomes took up a merry song and went back about their baking. The old Gnome king smiled and wiped away his tears.

"Good," he said as he walked over to a small table nearby. "Now that that's settled," he said, his voice catching in his throat, "please sit with me. Be at ease. We're all friends here, or I hope we can be."

Two Gnomes pulled up a stool for me. I could tell they were still frightened out of their wits, but they smiled as best they could. Other Gnomes served their king and I the finest looking selection of cakes, tarts, and cookies that I'd ever seen. Another Gnome brought out a pot of tea. The Gnome king used a handkerchief to dry his face and blow his nose, still recovering from the fright I had given him, his gnarled old hands shaking.

"Please sir, help yourself, and be merry." The old Gnome poured himself a cup of tea and sampled a cream puff.

I tried a shortbread cookie, but didn't care much for it, too sweet for my taste, only taking a nibble. I smiled politely so as to not insult the old Gnome. Next, I tried a chocolate chip cookie as he called it.

It was wonderful. In fact, perhaps the best cookie I had ever tasted. As I raised the teacup to my lips to wash down the cookie, strangely, my vision blurred. Grew dark.

I felt myself falling.

I awoke flat on my back. No idea how long I'd been out.

What happened? I blinked to clear my fuzzy vision. I felt so weak. I couldn't move. I felt wet and hot.

"Ah, dear boy," said the Gnome king. "You've decided to rejoin us at last. For a while I feared that you'd never awake. That wouldn't do at all."

"What happened?" I asked.

"You ate one of our cookies, dear boy, and fell fast asleep," said the Gnome king, his voice caring and comforting.

"To sleep?" I said, my head still foggy.

"Yes, to sleep, of course," said the Gnome king. "It would have been quite a bother to get you on the tray had you not been fast asleep."

"Tray? What do you mean?" And then I realized that I was bound down, at chest, arms, wrists, and legs, and it felt as if the ground were moving.

"Who are you?" I said. "Tell me true."

"Why I'm a Black Elf, of course," he said, his voice cold as ice. "Brak Moon MacLintel, I am, Lord of Boodlebarrow and king of the upland Svarts."

"Oh, dear gods," I said. "Dear gods."

"No gods can save you now, dear boy," said the Svart king.

"What will you do with me?" I cried, still trying to clear my head and vision. "What madness is this?"

"Not madness, dear boy," said the Black Elf king. "Oh no, not madness at all. We're quite rational here. Everything planned and pondered. For now, we simply need more savory treats to munch on as we bake our next batch of cookies, so we're rolling you over to an oven for roasting. We waited until you were awake, as is our custom. We do so want to hear you scream."

What!? I blinked furiously until I could see straight. Some hero was I. Now I needed rescuing. My brothers would never let me live this down. I lifted my head. Looked about in horror and disbelief. Not far away, I saw old Thom the cobbler strapped down to a huge metal baking tray that sat atop a wheeled cart. They had him covered in their liquid chocolate. Dear gods, he must have eaten those cakes after all. Thom's face contorted in horror and poured with sweat. His mouth was moving as he looked at me, his eyes pleading, but only gibberish came out his mouth. I hoped my brothers would arrive in time to save old Thom, for surely they'd be out in force to find me by now. And they knew exactly where I'd be.

A group of Elves wheeled Thom's cart up to a great oven, carefully opened the door, shielding themselves from the flames that briefly erupted outward, and with a concerted shove -- slid Thom's tray straight in.

Thom screamed as they slammed the big metal door shut.

He screamed and screamed some more.

Those were the most horrible sounds I'd ever heard. What pain he must have felt. What agony. Unbearable.

The Alders would make those damnable Black Elves pay tenfold for that unspeakable crime. We'd stick every Elf in the tribe atop pikes. Hang them from the village palisades for the birds to pick at, if even they would have them.

My cart came to a halt, banging into an oven door. I felt the heat rolling off of it before they even thought to open it. Teal would burst into the cavern at any moment, sword swinging. Torman beside him. Tribor too. And all our men with them. Where in Helheim were they?

The Black Elves pulled open the oven door. Heat beyond imagining poured over my feet.

Oh, dear gods, no! This can't be happening.

"Wait, wait, please don't do this," I begged, stalling. "There are things I must tell you. My family will reward you dearly for my safe return. Just wait a moment and let's talk. It will be worth your while. Please don't kill me."

The old Elf king leaned over the cart. "Dear boy, whatever you do, don't forget to scream," it said with an evil grin as they pushed my tray into the oven.

END

Thanks for reading *The Keblear Horror.* I hope that you enjoyed it, and that you will consider taking a few moments to return to where you purchased it

(http://www.glenngthater.com/thank-you.html)

 to leave a brief review. Reviews help my work gain visibility and provide me with valuable feedback about what my readers enjoyed and didn't enjoy about the story.

To be notified about my new book releases and any special offers or discounts regarding my books, please join my free mailing list here: http://eepurl.com/vwubH

Thank you again, and please check out the other books in the Harbinger of Doom series.

ABOUT GLENN G. THATER

For more than twenty-five years, Glenn G. Thater has written works of fiction and historical fiction that focus on the genres of epic fantasy and sword and sorcery. His published works of fiction include the first ten volumes of the *Harbinger of Doom* saga: *Gateway to Nifleheim*; *The Fallen Angle*; *Knight Eternal*; *Dwellers of the Deep*; *Blood, Fire, and Thorn*; *Gods of the Sword*; *The Shambling Dead*; *Master of the Dead*; *Shadow of Doom*; *Wizard's Toll*; the novella, *The Gateway*; and the novelette, *The Hero and the Fiend*.

Mr. Thater holds a Bachelor of Science degree in Physics with concentrations in Astronomy and Religious Studies, and a Master of Science degree in Civil Engineering, specializing in Structural Engineering. He has undertaken advanced graduate study in Classical Physics, Quantum Mechanics, Statistical Mechanics, and Astrophysics, and is a practicing licensed professional engineer specializing in the multidisciplinary alteration and remediation of buildings, and the forensic investigation of building failures and other disasters.

Mr. Thater has investigated failures and collapses of numerous structures around the United States and internationally. Since 1998, he has been a member of the American Society of Civil Engineers' Forensic Engineering Division (FED), is a Past Chairman of that Division's Executive Committee and FED's Committee on Practices to Reduce Failures. Mr. Thater is a LEED (Leadership in Energy and Environmental Design) Accredited Professional and has testified as an expert witness in the field of structural engineering before the Supreme Court of the State of New York.

Mr. Thater is an author of numerous scientific papers, magazine articles, engineering textbook chapters, and countless engineering reports. He has lectured across the United States and internationally on such topics as the World Trade Center collapses, bridge collapses, and on the construction and analysis of the dome of the United States Capitol in Washington D.C.

CONNECT WITH GLENN G. THATER ONLINE

Glenn G. Thater's Website:
http://www.glenngthater.com

To be notified about new book releases and any special offers or discounts regarding Glenn's books, please join his mailing list here: http://eepurl.com/vwubH

BOOKS BY GLENN G. THATER

THE HARBINGER OF DOOM SAGA
GATEWAY TO NIFLEHEIM
THE FALLEN ANGLE
KNIGHT ETERNAL
DWELLERS OF THE DEEP
BLOOD, FIRE, AND THORN
GODS OF THE SWORD
THE SHAMBLING DEAD
MASTER OF THE DEAD
SHADOW OF DOOM
WIZARD'S TOLL
VOLUME 11+ *forthcoming*

THE HERO AND THE FIEND
(A novelette set in the Harbinger of Doom universe)

THE GATEWAY
(A novella length version of *Gateway to Nifleheim*)

HARBINGER OF DOOM
(Combines *Gateway to Nifleheim* and *The Fallen Angle* into a single volume)

THE DEMON KING OF BERGHER
(A short story set in the Harbinger of Doom universe)

THE KEBLEAR HORROR
(A short story set in the Harbinger of Doom universe)

Visit Glenn G. Thater's website at http://www.glenngthater.com for the most current list of my published books.

www.ingramcontent.com/pod-product-compliance
Lightning Source LLC
Chambersburg PA
CBHW020323150626
46552CB00022B/3179

* 9 7 8 0 6 9 2 6 5 1 1 3 1 *